Adventures of Robin Hood

Retold by
ELEANOR GRAHAM VANCE

Illustrated by
JAY HYDE BARNUM

Prepared under the supervision of
JOSETTE FRANK, Children's Book Adviser of the
Child Study Association of America

Copyright 1953 by Random House, Inc.
All rights reserved under International and Pan-American Copyright Conventions.
Published in New York by Random House, Inc. and simultaneously in
Toronto, Canada by Random House of Canada Limited.
Library of Congress Catalog Card Number: 53-6291.
Manufactured in the U. S. A.

RANDOM HOUSE, INC., NEW YORK

LONG, long ago, when Henry the Second was king of England, his country had many troubles. The king's sons were warring against their father, and although the wealthy noblemen lived in luxury in their great castles, most of the people of the land were poor, and some were close to starving. A man could become an outlaw without wanting to, for the laws were so strict and unfair that one could break them almost without knowing it.

A certain nobleman of the kingdom, William Fitzooth, Earl of Huntington, did what he could to help the people who lived near him. He and his wife brought up their son, Robert, to be kind and thoughtful to everybody. The Earl also taught Robert all he knew of archery, and father and son loved to roam through their forests to hunt. At home, they would set up a target to see which one could speed the gray arrows most surely to the mark.

Their neighbor, Lord Lacy, often joined in this game, and sometimes he brought with him his pretty daughter, Marian, who was a year or two younger than Robert. Since Lord Lacy had no son, he had taught his daughter the archer's skill, and she and Robert were friendly rivals with the bow.

But sad times were to come for the Fitzooths. Earl William had been so generous that by the time his son was fourteen, he had given away most of his money to help his poor neighbors. Then some of the greedy lords, who hated him just because he was good to poor people, plotted against Earl William, seized his lands, and threw him into prison. His wife, overcome by worry, died a few weeks after her husband was taken away, and when her husband heard this sad news in his prison cell he, too, fell ill and died.

Lord Lacy took Robert to live in his castle, and Marian did her best to make the boy forget his grief. The two became better friends than ever, but Robert missed the hunts with his father, and even Marian and her parents could not make up this loss to him. Also, he wished to find some way to make a living.

When he was fifteen, he asked permission to go by himself to the famous Nottingham Fair where archers came from many miles around to try their skill.

"My father promised me that I might go when I reached fifteen," he told Lord Lacy. "We thought then that I should go only for the love of sport, and to try my skill, but now I have a better reason. They say the Sheriff of Nottingham will give the best archers places among the King's Foresters."

"But if you become a Forester, you would have to leave here!" cried Marian.

"Yes," said Robert, "but I can't live on your family's kindness forever. Now that my father's lands have been taken from me, I must find some way to earn my living. And I can think of nothing better than serving the king in the freedom of the greenwood."

Marian sighed at the thought of losing her friend, but her father understood the boy's feeling.

"You are right, Rob," he said. "You can whittle as good an arrow as any man, and speed it to its mark better than most. You are as tall as a man, and I like your manly spirit. You may go to the Fair."

So it was that on a fine spring morning Robert took up his good yew bow and a quiver full of arrows and set out on foot for Nottingham. He was glad that his path lay through Sherwood Forest, for he loved the woods. As he walked along he whistled a merry tune that seemed to match the springtime songs of the birds.

Suddenly he noticed a sound that came not from the birds or any greenwood creature. It was the noise of laughter and the rough voices of men. Turning aside from the path, Rob saw a group of fifteen men gathered around a fire where they were roasting venison for their lunch.

"The King's Foresters!" said Rob to himself. "Maybe I'll be one of them soon."

Looking on with admiration as the men gobbled up the venison

and washed it down with mugs of ale, Rob stood staring until one
of the men noticed him.

"Well, youngster!" called the man rudely. "Where do you think you are going with that longbow?"

"To Nottingham Fair," said Rob pleasantly enough, though he felt his face grow hot, because he saw that the Forester was making fun of him. "I mean to try my luck in the archers' tournament, and then perhaps I, too, may be a King's Forester."

At this such a shout of laughter went up that Rob wished he had said nothing.

"You a Forester of the King!" said one man. "You are nothing but a lad."

"Are you big enough to draw the bowstring?" taunted another. And all the men joined in with rough jokes at the boy's expense.

Stung to the heart and anxious to prove himself, Rob cried out, "Choose me a mark! Choose me a mark, and I bet I'll hit it!"

"Choose your own mark," shouted the leader of the men in green. "But I'll bet twenty pieces of silver that you won't hit it."

"Done!" cried Robert, and he looked about him for a target. Through the trees in a little glade fully a hundred rods away, some deer were grazing. "I'll shoot the hart at the head of yon herd," he said.

"Shoot away," said the Forester contemptuously, "but no arrow of yours will touch the hart."

Robert said nothing, but fitted the arrow to the bowstring, took careful aim, and let the arrow go. Faster than a bird's flight, it skimmed to the mark. The graceful hart leaped in the air, then fell to the ground, while the others in the herd, startled, vanished into the forest.

Flushed with success and expecting that the men would now prove more friendly, Rob turned to them saying, "I've won the bet."

To his amazement they were looking at him angrily, and muttering among themselves: "Who is this upstart lad?" "We'd better teach him a thing or two."

The leader stepped forward. "Speak of no bet," he said harshly. "You have killed a deer in King Henry's forest. You have broken the law. Be off with you before we turn you over to the Sheriff to cut off your ears!"

Rob started to protest, then saw there was no use. He turned back to the forest path when suddenly an arrow whizzed past his ear. The leader of the Foresters had shot at him! But his hand was unsteady either from anger or from too much ale, and the arrow missed Rob's head by a good two inches.

The boy whirled around, fitting his arrow to the bow. There was

only one way to defend himself in this treacherous attack. Before another man could reach for his bow, Rob let fly his arrow, and the Head Forester fell to the ground. Some of the men scrambled for their bows, others sat as if turned to stone, but Rob was running like a deer through the forest. They would surely kill him if they could! He must put a safe distance between himself and those Foresters. He ran and

ran until he came to a little thicket that would make a good hiding place. There he threw himself down, panting for breath. At first he was sick with horror at what he had done. He had slain a man! But soon he began to think of the great change that had come upon his life.

"An outlaw!" he thought in bewilderment. "Now I am an outlaw! If I go to Nottingham now, they will cut off my ears. I shall have to stay here in Sherwood Forest where I can hide."

It was natural that he should first think only of his own safety, but as the days went by, he found there were others like himself in the forest—men who had become outlaws by killing a deer for their starving families. Some had been thrown out of their homes and had lost all their possessions to greedy and evil overlords. Hiding in caves or rough shelters they had built for themselves, they lived as they could. Robert found them good friends, and they soon took him into their band.

"But you must have a new name," said one who was called Will Stutely. "Robert is a good name, but let us give it more of a greenwood sound. We shall call you Robin. And here is a suit of Lincoln green for you to wear, and a hood to keep your head warm when the winds of winter blow. Yes, a hood! And that will give us the rest of your name. Robin Hood! How do you like it?"

"Robin Hood," the boy repeated. "It has an honest sound. When any one of you has a chance, I should like to send word to Lord Lacy and his daughter Marian so they will not worry about me. Just tell them that Robert Fitzooth has become Robin Hood and lives in Sherwood Forest, and ask them to keep my secret."

As time went by the other outlaws turned to Robin more and more for advice. It was not only that they respected his skill with the longbow but also that they looked up to him because of his courage and kindness.

"Our good land of England suffers because too many rich noblemen rob and plunder the common people," he told the men. "Until the day when we can get better laws, we must do what we can for the poor. For every lord who is kind as my father was kind, there are a dozen selfish ones who grow rich and powerful by taking what belongs to those who work on their land. Men like the Sheriff of Nottingham are on the side of the wicked lords. Let us do what we can to right these wrongs. Let us rob only those who have robbed others, and let us share what we get with those who are in need."

Finding good sense in all that he said and did, the outlaws soon made Robin their leader. The band grew larger, and all over the country, people spoke of Robin Hood and his men. Rich and greedy men feared to travel through the forest, for they knew their money would be taken from them, but honest, simple folk knew that Robin was their friend and would help them when he could.

By the time Robin was twenty, he had more than a hundred good bowmen in his company. Wherever he went in the forest his men were not far off. He had only to blow his horn and they would come quickly to help him.

One day, as he was about to cross a brook, he saw a stranger who was uncommonly tall—fully seven feet in height. They met on the long narrow bridge, and neither would move to let the other pass.

Robin drew an arrow from his quiver, but the stranger said, "If you but touch the bow string, I'll knock you off the bridge."

Robin replied, "But I could send an arrow through your proud heart before you could strike one blow."

"The words of a coward," said the tall man. "You stand there armed with a longbow, and I have nothing but a staff in my hand."

"I scorn the name of coward," said Robin. "So I'll set my bow aside and get me a staff like yours."

He stepped back to a thicket of trees near the brook and cut a good oak staff. Then he ran back onto the bridge calling, "See my tough staff? Now we'll battle it out here on the bridge. Whichever one of us knocks the other into the brook shall win. Let's go!"

"With all my heart!" cried the stranger, and they began to battle with their long staffs. First Robin gave the tall man such a bang that his bones ached, but he shouted, "I'll give as good as I get," and with that, he cracked Robin on the head. Robin was furious, and fought harder than ever. Blow followed blow, thick and fast, until suddenly the stranger with one mighty stroke tumbled Robin into the brook!

"Where are you now, good fellow?" the stranger called, laughing.

"Good faith," answered Robin, "in the water! You are a brave soul, and we'll fight no longer, for you have won the day."

And pulling himself up on the bank, Robin put his bugle-horn to his lips and blew a loud blast. Out of the woods his men came running.

"Good master," cried Will Stutely, "you are wet to the skin! What has happened?"

"No matter," said Robin. "This tall lad here has tumbled me in."

"Then he shall go in, too," cried the men, and they laid hands on the stranger, but Robin stopped them.

"Wait!" he cried. "He's a stout fellow," and turning to the man on the bridge he added, "Have no fear, friend. These are my bowmen. If you will join us, we will dress you in Lincoln green, and I'll make you an archer."

"Here's my hand," said the man. "My name is John Little, and I'll serve you with all my heart."

"John Little!" exclaimed Will Stutely, looking the seven-foot man

up and down. "Then let us change his name. From now on he shall be known as Little John."

At this a shout of laughter went up, and Little John joined in as heartily as any. Then the party made their way to the camping place and dined royally on venison and wine. After the feast, a suit of Lincoln green was brought out for the newcomer. He was presented with a longbow, and Robin told him, "You will be an archer along with the best of us. We eat well and we sleep well in the greenwood, and you shall be one of us."

So it was that Little John became one of Robin Hood's merry men, and a true and faithful friend he proved to be. Soon he was second only to the leader in archery, and Robin looked upon him as his right-hand man. Friends of Little John also joined the band—Gilbert of the White Hand and funny little Much, the Miller's Son.

One day Little John, Much, and Gilbert brought a shabby stranger before Robin.

"Here is a sad-looking knight we found riding alone through the forest."

"Welcome, Sir Knight," said Robin. "You are just in time to have dinner with us."

After an excellent meal of venison, swan, and pheasant, Robin

asked the sad knight how much money he had with him.

"Nothing but ten shillings," said the knight.

"Can a knight be so poor?" asked Robin.

"He speaks the truth, master," said Little John, who was looking through the knight's belongings.

"Have you wasted your money?" Robin asked the knight. "Speak freely to me, and perhaps I can help you. I am Robin Hood."

"I have heard much good of you," said the knight. "My name is Sir Richard of the Lea. No, I have not wasted my money. My son unfortunately killed a man by accident in a tournament. In order to pay his fine, I borrowed money from a rich abbot. I am supposed to pay the debt today, but I have not been able to raise the money. So the abbot will take my land. That is why you see me so sorrowful."

"Have you no friends?" asked Robin.

"When I was rich I had many, but now that I am poor I cannot find them."

"How much do you owe the abbot?" Robin asked.

"Four hundred pounds," answered Sir Richard.

Then Robin gave a few whispered commands to his men, and they went off. In a few minutes they returned, Little John carrying a bag of money, Gilbert and Much bringing many yards of fine cloth.

"Sir Richard," said Robin, "here is four hundred pounds so that you may pay your debt, and some cloth to make new clothes for you."

"And a fresh horse, master," whispered little Much, the Miller's Son.

"Yes, yes, give him a good horse," said Robin, and immediately his men brought forth a beautiful gray charger.

Sir Richard's eyes filled with tears as he saw the kindness of the outlaws, but he asked only, "When can I repay this debt?"

"A year from today," answered Robin. "Take good care of yourself, Sir Richard. England has need of knights like you. If there were more like you, that silly, evil man would not be Sheriff of Nottingham, for it is only a few scheming lords who keep him there."

Robin sent some of his men to escort Sir Richard on his way, and the knight rode off happily.

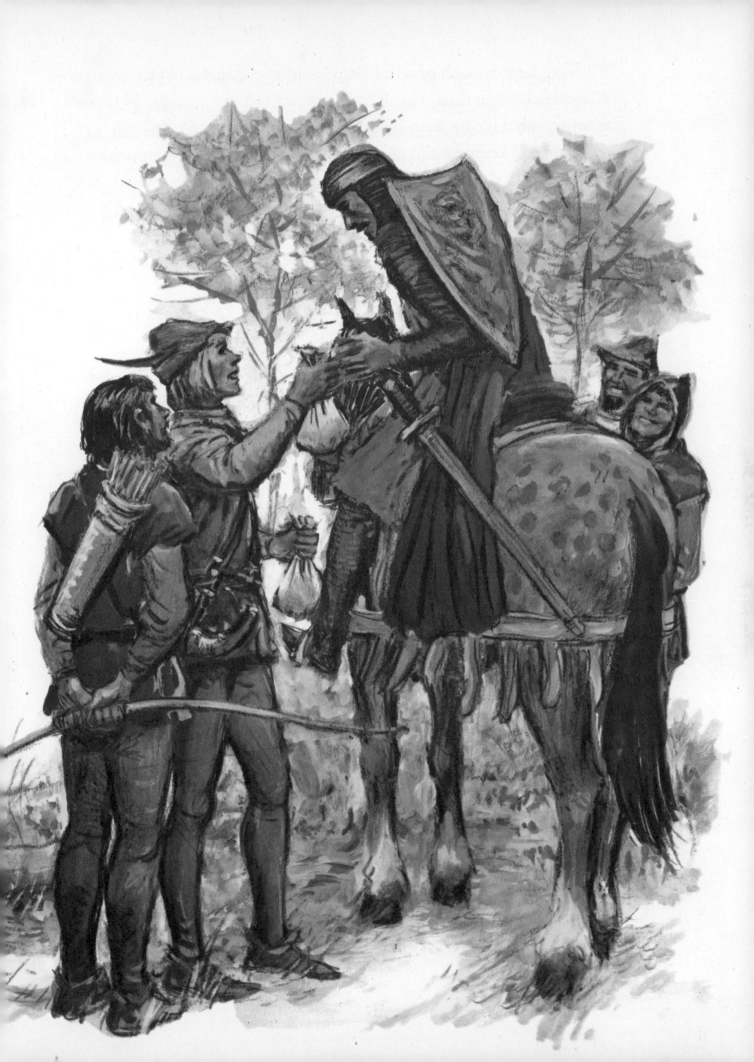

Not long after Sir Richard's visit, Robin was walking alone through Sherwood Forest when he saw a young man dressed all in red. The gaily dressed stranger had just lifted his bow to take aim at a herd of deer, and in a moment his arrow brought down the best buck in the herd.

"Well shot!" cried Robin. "How would you like to join my company of men?"

"Get along with you," said the stranger rudely, "unless you want a fight."

Instantly Robin Hood bent his bow to take aim at this man in red, but the stranger was taking aim at him at the same moment.

"Wait!" cried Robin, admiring the bold spirit of the man. "If we both shoot, one of us will surely be killed. Let's try each other with our swords."

And a beautiful bit of swordplay followed. Robin was so busy admiring the style of the stranger that before long a sudden stroke brought the blood trickling down Robin's face.

"What a swordsman you are!" he cried. "Tell me your name."

"I'm Will Gamwell," said the stranger. "Things have been going badly with me. The Sheriff of Nottingham tricked me into killing a man, and so I am an outlaw. I am searching this forest for a cousin of mine. Some call him Robin Hood."

"Will Gamwell, my cousin!" cried Robin. "Why didn't you say so in the first place? I am Robin Hood."

What a happy reunion there was then! The two had not seen each other since their boyhood, and they had much to talk about.

"The poor people of England have few to help them," said Will. "I have heard much of you and your merry men. You are outlaws like me, but you do more good than most of those who live in castles."

"Yes," said Robin. "No man of mine has ever harmed the farmers, for we know that they grow food for the people to eat. We always protect women, and those weaker than ourselves. Any poor man may walk safely through these woods. But woe to those who have grown rich by robbing the poor!"

"I would like to join your band," said Will.

Before Robin could answer Litttle John came running up.

"Where have you been so long, master?" he asked.

"I met this man who has beaten me in a sword fight."

"Then I'll have a bout with him," cried Little John, "and see if he can beat me."

"Oh no," said Robin quickly, "for he is to become a new member of our band. This is Will Gamwell, my own cousin, and he will be my chief man next to you, Little John."

"Welcome," said Little John heartily. "But master, how shall we call him?"

"Let's see," said Robin thoughtfully. "How about calling him Will Scarlet? Then his name will match his bright clothing."

This name seemed to please both Will and Little John. Much, the Miller's Son, came along just then; and he, too, approved of the new man and his new name.

The four friends started back to the outlaws' gathering place, stopping to hunt on the way, for Robin reported that their provisions were low since their feast with Sir Richard. When Robin spied a herd of deer grazing, his three men all shot at once, and each one brought down a deer.

"Fine shooting!" Robin exclaimed. "I'd ride a hundred miles to see a man who could match any one of you in archery."

Will Scarlet laughed heartily and said, "You needn't ride so far, Robin. I know a monk who lives at Fountain's Abbey—Friar Tuck by name—and he can shoot better than we have done."

"Then I shall neither eat nor drink till I see Friar Tuck," said Robin. "You three, carry the deer back to the men. Tell them to send back for the buck Will killed when I met him. Get them to start preparing the venison, and then follow after me if you like."

With his usual delight in a new adventure, Robin set off in the

direction of Fountain's Abbey. After a while he came to a broad stream. Now Robin was wearing a coat of mail under his suit of Lincoln green, and he did not want to get it wet. So he walked along the bank looking for a shallow place where he might wade across. Suddenly he bumped right into a stout, jolly-looking friar who was also walking along the bank, chuckling to himself. This man was dressed in long, flowing robes. His big round face was as red and shiny as a polished apple, and his eyes twinkled merrily. His head was shaved all except for a little fringe of curly black hair growing around the edge like a crown. Robin decided to make use of this friar, so he asked him to carry him across the stream. The holy man agreed good-naturedly, but no sooner were they on the other side than he said, "Now, my fine young man, one good turn deserves another. I carried you over, but I want to be on the other side. I shall have to ask you to carry me back."

Thinking to himself that this game could go on forever, Robin carried the heavy friar across and then said, "Holy man, you have taught me to do unto others as I would have them do unto me. Now you must practice what you preach, and carry me back."

Without a word, the friar took Robin on his back and waded into the water. But halfway across, he suddenly stopped, tossed his burden *kersplash!* into the water, and walked calmly to the bank.

With much puffing and splashing Robin gained the bank and cried out angrily, "Holy man or not, now we must fight," and he pulled out his sword. The friar was so quick with his own sword that neither man could win. Up and down the bank they leapt nimbly, their swords

flashing in the sunlight and clanging with so much noise that all the birds flew away to the shelter of the forest. After several hours of fighting, Robin panted, "Just let me blow three blasts on my horn!"

"Go ahead," said the friar. "I hope you blow till your eyes fall out."

But as soon as the sound of the horn had died away in the distance, as many as fifty men in Lincoln green came running out of the woods.

"Whose men are these?" asked the friar in surprise.

"Mine," said Robin.

"Well, then," said the friar calmly, "since I let you blow your horn, will you let me put my fingers in my mouth and whistle three times?"

"Whistle away," said Robin.

In answer to the friar's whistle, fifty dogs came running up.

"Here's a dog for every one of your men," said the friar, and immediately the dogs started after the merry men. Little John and the others snatched up their bows and began to shoot, but a strange sight it was, for the dogs had been so well trained that they dodged the arrows, watched where they landed, and brought them back in their mouths.

Then Will Scarlet came running up and shouted, "Call off your dogs, Friar Tuck."

"Friar Tuck!" exclaimed Robin. "Then this is the man I was looking for! I should have guessed it. He is all that you said, Will, and we must have him join our band."

"Well," said Friar Tuck, whistling to his dogs who gathered round him, "I've lived at Fountain's Abbey for seven years, and never, until today, have I met a man I would follow. You must be Robin Hood, and I'm sorry for the ducking I gave you."

"Then prove it by joining us," said Robin with a laugh, "but what shall we do with all your dogs?"

"They take care of themselves in the forest, just as your men do. If I need them I whistle, and if they need me they come to me. One part of the forest is as good as another to them."

Then the whole band began making their way back through Sherwood to the place where their dinner of roast venison and pheasant was waiting. A fine dinner it was, and the merry men spent that evening and the next day in games and tests of archery skill as a sort of welcome to Will Scarlet and Friar Tuck.

So time went by, and just a year had passed since the visit of Sir Richard of the Lea.

"Do you think he will come today to repay his debt?" asked Much.

"I am sure of it," said Little John. "The sun is still high in the sky."

"Well, go forth and find some guests to have dinner with us," said Robin. "You and Much and Will Scarlet, see what kind of travelers you can find."

Very soon Little John, Much, and Will returned with two men. Robin's men were smiling, but their guests were not.

"These are very special travelers, master," they told Robin.

"Yes," spoke one of the strangers, "we are close friends of the Sheriff of Nottingham, and it will go hard with you, Robin Hood, when he finds your men have stopped us."

"Well, well," said Robin pleasantly. "How does the Sheriff these days? Does he still have one set of laws for rich people and another set for poor people?"

"We are on an errand for the Sheriff," said one of the two newcomers. "You had better let us go."

"How much money do you carry in your coffers?" asked Robin.

"Only twenty marks," answered the Sheriff's friends.

"If you have no more than that, you need it, and I shall not take a penny," said Robin. "Look and see, Little John."

But when Little John shook out the travelers' money on the ground, there was more than eight hundred pounds!

"Only twenty marks!" Robin exclaimed. "How do you account for this?"

"It is the Sheriff's money," one of the travelers explained sullenly. "We were taking it to a certain lord's castle for safekeeping."

"Because the Sheriff has no right to it and is afraid some of those from whom it was taken might come and get it back? Well, you can leave it *here* for safekeeping. Now you may eat and drink and then be on your way."

The travelers seemed to have little appetite and were in a great hurry to leave Robin Hood. Scarcely were they out of sight when Will Stutely came running up to say that Sir Richard of the Lea and some of his followers were approaching.

After pleasant greetings, Sir Richard explained that his people and his lands were doing well and he had come to repay his debt to Robin.

"I am sorry to get here so late in the day," he said, "but we came upon a poor yeoman in trouble, and we stayed to right his wrongs."

"Those are words we like to hear," said Robin. "Anyone who helps a poor yeoman is a friend to Robin Hood and his men."

"I have here the four hundred pounds you so kindly lent me," said Sir Richard, "with twenty marks added for your courtesy."

"No, Sir Richard," said Robin gently. "Your debt has already been paid—and paid double. From the men of the rascally Sheriff of Nottingham we have just taken eight hundred pounds. We should like you to take half of that—four hundred pounds—and see if you can find those to whom it rightfully belongs."

"That I will gladly do," said the knight, "but I am also ready to pay my debt."

"No," said Robin. "If all men did as much good with their money as you do, there would not be much work for my merry men and me. But what are your men carrying?"

"A present for you and your men," said Sir Richard. "If you won't

let me pay you the money, you must at least accept this gift of a hundred bows and a hundred sheaves of arrows."

"Gladly," said Robin, and all the men crowded round to admire the gift. The longbows were beautifully made, and every arrow was set with peacock's feathers and notched with silver. No gift could have pleased the merry men more, and they and Sir Richard's followers vowed to be friends and to help one another always—vows that were kept on both sides.

One morning, a few days later, Little John and Much noticed a well-dressed young man walking through the forest, murmuring sadly every few steps, "Alas and alack!" He carried with him a minstrel's harp, but he played no music.

Since they were curious to know why he was so sad, they stopped him and took him to Robin Hood.

"Why so sorrowful, young man?" the forest leader asked.

"Yesterday I was happy," said the stranger. "I was to marry fair Ellen. But her father owes money to the Sheriff of Nottingham, and the Sheriff wants Ellen to marry someone rich so he will surely get his money. The Sheriff and her father have arranged for her to marry a wealthy old knight, and my heart is broken."

"If the maiden loves you, why don't you fight for her?" asked Robin?

"She loves me with all her heart," said the stranger. "Here is the ring I have kept for seven years to give her on our wedding day. But the knight she is to marry is too old for me to fight. He's even older than Ellen's father. I could knock him down with one finger, and that I must not do. Besides, the wedding is all arranged."

"Then we must help you," Robin decided. "What is your name?"

"Alan-a-Dale."

"And can you make music on that harp?"

"That I can, but right now my heart is too heavy," answered Alan.

"What will you give me if I arrange for you to marry your true love?"

"I have no money," said Alan, "but I will be your true servant if Ellen can be my wife."

"A minstrel to sing songs of the daring adventures of my merry men is just what we need," said Robin. "We'll tell you about the time we rescued Will Stutely from hanging, and of my fight with Guy of Gisbourne, and many another tale, and you can put them into song. But now tell me——"

Alan told him sadly that Ellen's wedding to the old knight was to take place that very day at a church about five miles away. Quickly and carefully Robin told the men his plans. Then he borrowed Alan's harp and hurried to the church. There he found the bishop, but the wedding party had not yet arrived.

"What are you doing here?" asked the bishop as Robin ran up to him.

"I am a minstrel," said Robin, pointing to the harp he carried.

"Good," said the bishop. "Will you play for the wedding that is to take place here?"

"Not until I see the bride and groom," answered Robin.

"Here they come," said the bishop, and sure enough a strange procession on horseback was drawing near the church. First came a gray-bearded knight so old and weak that he could hardly sit on his horse. Then came his men gaily dressed in new and shining clothes for the occasion. Then, riding at her father's side and followed by a group of maidens, came a beautiful young girl who made Robin think of Maid Marian. There were tears in her blue eyes, but she held her head high and looked straight before her.

As the party dismounted at the church, Robin muttered, "Such a match as this cannot be."

"What did you say?" asked the bishop. "Why don't you start the music?"

"That I will," said Robin, but instead of playing the harp, he pulled out his horn and blew three blasts. Immediately, twenty-four archers, headed by Alan-a-Dale, came running up. Quickly Alan handed Robin his bow, and the armed men stood there awaiting their leader's command.

At sight of Alan, the fair Ellen had blushed rosy red and then turned very pale. Others of the company, amazed at the sudden interruption, stood silent, waiting to see what was going to happen. Even the bishop was too surprised to speak, and Robin's voice rang out low and clear as he turned to speak to Ellen.

"Here is Alan-a-Dale, your true love," he said, "and I am here with these good men of mine to see that you and he are married. Friar Tuck, will you marry these two?"

By now the people had crowded into the church—all except the old knight and his men and Ellen's father, who stood just outside the door with Will Stutely and a few other of Robin's men to watch over them. Friar Tuck read the service, with none of his usual joking, because he

realized what a solemn moment this was. Robin Hood gave the bride away.

When the wedding was over, the whole party went happily back to Sherwood Forest.

"But how shall we live in the woods?" asked Ellen.

"That will be easy," said Robin. "My men have many a cave and many a cottage in the greenwood. We will turn over a little place to you and Alan. You can keep house as well in the forest as in the town."

That night the forest heard sweet music as the outlaws gathered around the fire after the wedding feast to sing and to listen to Alan-a-Dale's harp. Alan had much to tell them about what was going on in the world outside Sherwood Forest. Most of the men did not even know that King Henry had died.

"When good Richard the Lion-Hearted became king," said Alan, "we thought that all might go better for our poor people. But now he is off on a crusade to the Holy Land, and things are worse than ever. Prince John, his evil brother, is ruling in Richard's place, and they say he plots to seize his brother's throne. He cares for nothing but more money and more power. He squeezes money from the poor to give to the rich to buy their favor. And now, since the poor have nothing more to give him, he must start on the rich. When Lord Lacy died, Prince John seized his lands and——"

But here Robin Hood's face grew dark and he interrupted: "Lord Lacy dead! And what has become of Maid Marian?"

"She is living at the court in London, under the protection of Prince John. Safe enough, I guess, but with all her father's lands taken from her."

"May the Lion-Heart return quickly," said Robin, "and then we must do something about this. He is a good king, and I think he might even pardon outlaws when he knows that we are loyal to him and have tried to help his suffering people."

He said no more for he did not want to bring a sorrowful note into the wedding celebration, but his heart was troubled not only for Maid Marian but for all the good people of the land.

Now when word came to the Sheriff of Nottingham that Robin had interfered with Ellen's wedding to the old knight, he was so angry that

he journeyed to London to ask Prince John for help in capturing the outlaw.

"Why, what do you expect *me* to do?" asked the Prince. "Aren't *you* the Sheriff? Aren't you supposed to keep the laws? You had better find some way to trap this bold outlaw, else I may have need of a new sheriff."

So the Sheriff, angrier than ever, went back to Nottingham. He was worried by what Prince John had said. Since he was not a brave man, his thoughts soon turned to trickery. It occurred to him that if he should proclaim another shooting match, Robin Hood and his men might be tempted to appear there to try their luck.

"That's it!" he exclaimed. "I'll have a beautiful arrow made—with a silver shaft and a golden head. The best archer shall carry away the prize. This news will surely bring the outlaw out into the open where my men will outnumber his."

And sure enough, when news of the golden arrow traveled to Sherwood, Robin Hood was eager for all his men to try for it.

But a brave young man, David of Doncaster, stepped up to the leader and said, "Master, listen to me. I have heard that this is only a trick of the Sheriff's to get you into his clutches. None of us should stir from the greenwood."

"You have done well to keep your ears open," said Robin, "but now I am even more determined to try my skill in the Sheriff's match."

Then up spoke Little John. "I have a plan whereby we may all go to the match, and no one will know who we are: We'll leave our suits of Lincoln green here in the forest. One of us shall wear white, another red, another yellow, another blue. They will be expecting to see us in green, and they'll never guess who we are."

And so, dressed in many colors and mingling with the holiday crowd, the outlaws went to Nottingham. The Sheriff, on the lookout for men in Lincoln green, could not hide his disappointment.

"I thought Robin Hood would surely be here," he said. "He may be bold, but he's not bold enough to venture into Nottingham."

Overhearing these words, Robin's blood boiled. He longed to let the fat Sheriff know that he *was* there. In his bright red clothes, he made a handsome picture, but since he had dyed his hair and darkened his face with walnut juice, no one knew him.

As the archery went on, voices rose out of the crowd, cheering this favorite or that. "Blue jacket!" cried one. "Brown," cried another; while a third shouted, "Brave Yellow!" Yet another man said, "No, it's Red! Yon man in red has no equal here today."

And Robin, fine shot that he was, was better than all the rest, and carried off the golden arrow to Sherwood. There the outlaws gathered round, admiring the prize and telling one another of the day's adventures.

"Only one thing troubles me," said Robin. "I should dearly love to have the Sheriff know that I am the one who bore this arrow away."

"And he *shall* know," cried Little John. "Write a note, and I'll see that he gets it."

A shout of approval went up from the band.

And that was how it happened that as the Sheriff was seated at his dinner table that night, there came a strange interruption. He had swallowed his disappointment of the afternoon, and was boasting that Robin Hood was afraid to show his face in Nottingham. Suddenly, through the window, flashed an arrow. It came to rest in the big fat goose the Sheriff was about to carve. The Sheriff turned white with fear, and stood there shaking.

"It bears a message," cried one of the guests. "Take it and read."

With trembling hands the Sheriff unwrapped the message and read, "It was I, Robin Hood, who won the golden arrow."

Then the Sheriff's anger overflowed, for he realized that once again Robin had outwitted him.

A few weeks later, Robin Hood was walking alone in Sherwood Forest, thinking about the troubles of the people and wondering what he could do, when through the trees he saw a young man dressed in the costume of a court page. He was small and slender, and seemed to be having trouble trying to manage the sword and buckler, quiver and bow that he carried.

"Here is a lad looking for adventure, so I shall give him some," thought Robin, and stepping from behind a tree, he said in a fierce voice, "Halt!"

Immediately the young man's sword flashed out, and he cried, "Draw, and defend yourself!"

"A pretty spirit!" thought Robin, drawing his sword, and in the next few minutes he admired the quickness and cleverness of the page's swordplay. Now Robin would never fight seriously with one smaller than himself, and soon he let the lad give him a slight scratch on the wrist. At sight of the blood, the page dropped his sword and said, "Now perhaps you will let me go on my way."

"Not at all," said Robin pleasantly. "How would you like to join Robin Hood's band?"

"Robin Hood!" cried the boy. "Are you——Are you——?" and to Robin's amazement, the page burst into tears, saying between sobs, "Oh Robin, I came searching for you, and now I've wounded you!"

This was surely a girl's voice! Robin stared in amazement, and then said uncertainly, "Marian!"

Then they were both talking at once, and Marian was laughing and crying at the same time, but finally Robin understood that she had disguised herself as a page and had come looking for him because she could no longer bear to live at the court of Prince John.

"King Richard, on his way home from the Holy Land, has been taken prisoner by the Duke of Austria," Marian told Robin. "Our fair land of England has sent money for his ransom, but no one can tell when he will get home. And I feared Prince John would try to

force me to marry one of his favorite nobles. So, Robin, I came to find you."

"I have lain awake nights thinking of you, Marian," said Robin. "I would have carried you off to the greenwood long ago, only I thought our rough life was not fit for a maiden. But now Alan-a-Dale and his bride are happy here, and so will you be. I shall not press you to marry me. Stay in the cottage with Ellen and Alan-a-Dale until you are used to the ways of our outlaw life."

Marian looked as if it would not take her long to get used to those ways, but she said nothing. While Robin was talking, she pulled out a lacy handkerchief and bound his wrist to protect the scratch her sword had made. Together they made their way to the outlaws' gathering place, and another fine feast was held to welcome Maid Marian.

She and Ellen quickly became friends, and within a few days Marian felt more at home in the forest than she had in London.

Not long after that, it happened one morning that Robin saw a group of monks riding through the woods. Thinking they might carry money that would add to the outlaws' treasury, he walked boldly up to their leader and stopped him by snatching the horse's bridle.

"Sir Abbot," he said, "it pleases me to ask for your money. There are many people who have need of it."

"If you are Robin Hood," said the abbot, "then I must tell you that I have a message for you from the king."

"God save the king," said Robin, "and all that wish him well."

"Strange words from a traitor," said the abbot.

Robin's eyes darkened and he spoke sternly: "If you were not the king's messenger, you would be sorry for those words. For I tell you I am loyal to my king and his suffering people. I have never hurt any man who is honest and true, but only those who live on what should belong to others." Then his voice grew lighter and he added, "Come to dinner with my merry men, and we shall hear your message."

A wonderful feast was set before the abbot and his men. There were venison and trout and pheasant and wine, for Robin wished to honor his guests. Alan-a-Dale played the harp and sang, while Ellen and Marian sat near the fire.

When dinner was over and the abbot still had not said what his message was, Robin called his men to give a show of archery. They hung up wreaths of flowers and shot through them, and many times they used a slender sapling for a target, but so true were the archers that their arrows always split the sapling neatly.

"Such shooting I have never seen before," said the abbot. "If I could get you a pardon from the king, would you serve him well?"

"That I would!" cried Robin. "Men, what do you say?"

"Yes! Yes!" cried the men.

The abbot stood up straight and tall, and let the hood of his cloak fall back to reveal thick brown hair, dark eyes, and a strong sunburned face. Marian gave a little gasp. "The King!" she exclaimed, and came to kneel before the tall figure. After a moment of astonishment Robin, too, knelt before the man he had thought was an abbot. The whispered words, "He is King Richard," went quickly around the group of outlaws, and soon the whole company was kneeling.

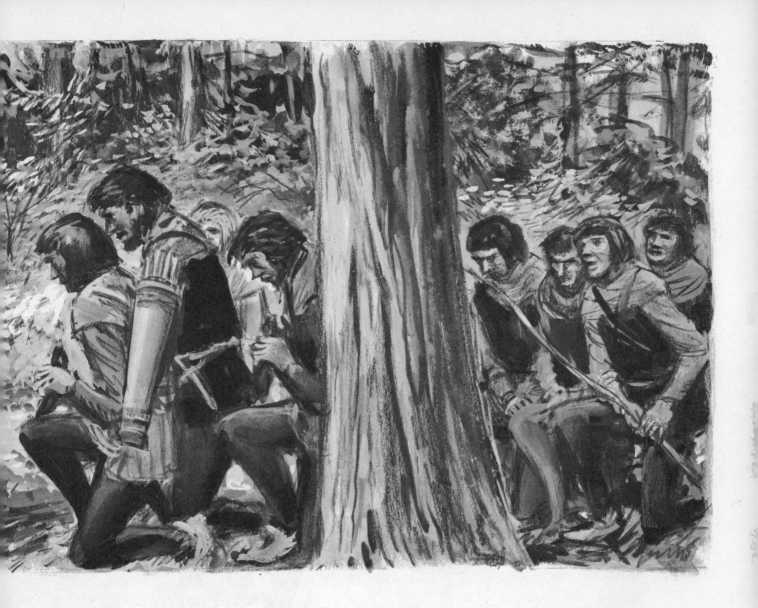

"Stand up and be free men," said King Richard, "for I give you all
a pardon. England has need of men like you. When I returned to
London, I heard many tales of your deeds, some good, some bad, and
so I came to see for myself. I know my people have suffered, and perhaps
you can help me to right the wrongs. Let us begin nearby: The Sheriff
of Nottingham has not served the people well. Can you suggest someone to take his place?"

With a smile, Robin Hood pointed to his right-hand man. "Little
John has strength and courage and a kind heart, Sire. He would be a
good sheriff."

"Then he shall be Sheriff of Nottingham," said the king.

Marian whispered something to Robin. He took her by the hand and together they stood before King Richard.

"Maid Marian, who is the king's ward at the court, is my true love. We ask a royal blessing on our marriage."

"You shall have it," said Richard. "Let us go to Nottingham for the wedding."

Amid great rejoicing, the whole company made ready for the journey. And when the wedding procession, with the King at its head, reached Nottingham, they received a warm welcome. The people were happy to know they would be rid of their evil sheriff and fairly treated by new laws under a just ruler.

The outlaws were outlaws no longer. All were assigned to serve their king in one way or another, and gave a good account of themselves. But to this day people speak of those times, and tell tales of the bold adventures of Robin Hood and his merry men in Sherwood Forest.

Adventures of
ROBIN HOOD